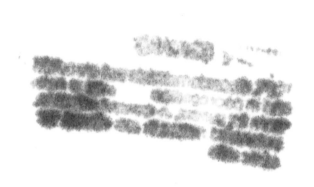

SWIMMING, DIVING, AND OTHER WATER SPORTS

by Jason Page

CONTENTS

r: Robert Walker
reader: Mike Hodge
owledgements: We would like to
Ian Hodge, Rosalind Beckman,
e Gaff, Ben Hubbard and Elizabeth
ans for their assistance.
ons by: John Alston
research: Image Select

Picture Credits:
t=top, b=bottom, l=left, r=right, OFC=outside front cover, OBC=outside back cover,
IFC=inside front cover; Allsport: IFC, 2/3t, 3b, 4/5t, 5b, 6/7 (main pic), 7tr, 8tr, 8/9c,
10/11t, 12/13 (main pic), 13tr, 15t, 16/17b, 18/19c, 20tl, 20/21 (main pic), 22l, 22/23t,
24/25 (main pic), 25t, 26/27b, 28/29t, 28/29b, 30/31c, 31tr; Daniel Berehulak/Getty
Images for FINA: 14/15b; Giuliano Bevilacqua/Rex Features: 16/17t; Adam Davy/
EMPICS Sport/PA Photos: 11b; Getty Images: OFC; Ronald Grant Archive: 19tr;
Reuters/Andy Clark SN/AA: 26/27t

ry and Archives Canada Cataloguing in Publication

Jason
Swimming, diving, and other water sports / Jason Page.

Olympic sports)
des index.
978-0-7787-4019-3 (bound).--ISBN 978-0-7787-4036-0 (pbk.)

1. Swimming--Juvenile literature. 2. Diving--Juvenile literature.
mpics--Juvenile literature. I. Title. II. Series: Page, Jason.
pic sports.

7.6.P33 2008   j797.2   C2008-900977-0

Library of Congress Cataloging-in-Publication Data
Page, Jason.
    Swimming, diving, and other water sports / Jason Page.
        p. cm. -- (The Olympic sports)
    Includes index.
    ISBN-13: 978-0-7787-4019-3 (rlb)
    ISBN-10: 0-7787-4019-6 (rlb)
    ISBN-13: 978-0-7787-4036-0 (pb)
    ISBN-10: 0-7787-4036-6 (pb)
    1. Swimming--Juvenile literature. 2. Diving--Juvenile literature. 3.
Olympics--Juvenile literature. I. Title. II. Series.
    GV837.6.P235 2008
    797--dc22
                                                              2008004956

Crabtree Publishing Company
www.crabtreebooks.com
1-800-387-7650

16A, 350 Fifth Ave.
3308,
York, NY

616 Welland Ave.
St. Catharines, ON
L2M 5V6

ished by Crabtree Publishing in 2008

Published in the United Kingdom © 2000 by ticktock
Entertainment Limited. Revised edition published in the United
Kingdom © 2008 by ticktock Media Ltd. The right of the author to
be identified as the author of this work has been asserted by him.

AQUATIC EVENTS

The National Aquatic Center in Beijing is nicknamed "water cube" after its square design. The building has a protective membrane, which covers it like an overcoat. The National Aquatic Center was built to host the aquatic events at the 2008 Games.

COOL!

The first-ever modern Olympic swimming event was the 100m freestyle, held in 1896. There were only three competitors, and the race was held not in a swimming pool, but in the the icy cold waters of the Bay of Zea, off the coast of Greece. Competitors simply dove off of a boat and swam to the shore! The race was won by a 19-year-old Hungarian sailor named Alfred Hajos.

SUPER STATS

There were over 1,200 athletes that took part in the aquatic events at the Beijing Olympics. Together they would fill two jumbo jets!

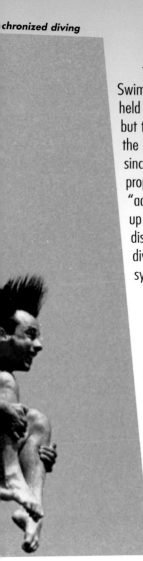

FOUR OF THE BEST

Swimming events were not held at the ancient Olympics, but they have been part of the modern Games ever since they began. The proper title of this sport is "aquatics," and it's made up of four separate disciplines: swimming, diving, water polo, and synchronized swimming.

AQUATIC FIRSTS

Several new events made their Olympic debut at the 2000 Games, including synchronized diving, shown here, and women's water polo.

OLYMPICS FACT FILE

The Olympic Games were first held in Olympia, in ancient Greece, around 3,000 years ago. They took place every four years until they were abolished in 393 A.D.

A Frenchman called Pierre de Coubertin (1863–1937) revived the Games, and the first modern Olympics were held in Athens in 1896.

The modern Games have been held every four years since 1896, except in 1916, 1940, and 1944, due to war. Special 10th-anniversary Games took place in 1906.

The symbol of the Olympic Games is five interlocking colored rings. Together, they represent the five original continents from which athletes came to compete in the Games.

GOLDEN GREATS

chael Phelps (USA) is the greatest swimmer ever seen at the Olympic mes. In the 2008 Olympics in Beijing, he won a total of eight gold medals. record is unmatched by any other swimmer at one Olympic Games.

Michael Phelps (USA)

50-METER FREESTYLE

The 50m freestyle covers just one length of the pool, making it the shortest and fastest of all the swimming races.

STRONG SWIMMER

In 1988, the Men's 50m freestyle was won by Matt Biondi (USA). Between 1984 and 1992, Biondi swam away with eight golds, two silvers, and a bronze.

Amy Van Dyken (USA)

ANIMAL OLYMPIANS

The gold medal for sprint swimming in the animal kingdom goes to the mighty sailfish. With a top speed of 68 MPH (110 km/h), this super-fast fish would finish the 50m freestyle in just 1.6 seconds!

TOUGH COMPETITION

Amy Van Dyken is the first American woman to win four gold medals in one Olympic Games. In 1996, she won gold in the 50m and 100m freestyle as well as and the medley and freestyle relay events. She went to Sydney four years later and won another two golds in the relays.

DID YOU KNOW?

An Olympic 50m freestyle champion swims at a top speed of about 4.97 MPH (8 km/h) —that's about twice as fast as your normal walking pace.

An Olympic swimming pool is 5.9 feet (1.8m) deep—that's deep enough to go over the head of an average adult.

The 50m event (or 50-yards, as it was then known) first appeared at the Olympic Games in 1904. It was not held again until 1988—84 years later.

LEARN TO CRAWL

freestyle races, any stroke can used—but swimmers always oose the front crawl because the fastest stroke. In the nt crawl, one arm goes over swimmer's head while the er is pushed down through water. At the same time, swimmer kicks his or her s quickly up and down— to six kicks per arm stroke.

Alexander Popov (RUS)

POPOV'S PRIDE OF PLACE

Alexander Popov (RUS) won both the 50m and the 100m freestyle at the 1992 and the 1996 Olympics. In 2000, he won the silver medal for the 100m.

Even short hair creates water resistance and slows swimmers down. That's why most swimmers wear swimming caps.

Swimmers wear goggles to protect their eyes from chemicals in the water.

Swim suits are made of light, flexible materials, including Teflon—also used to make non-stick frying pans!

DID YOU KNOW?

The 1984 Women's 100m freestyle final was a dead heat. Both swimmers were awarded gold medals.

The swimming events at the Olympics in 1900 included a 200m obstacle race!

Women competed in swimming events at the Olympics for the first time in 1912.

MEN'S RECORDS – WORLD: 100m: Eamon Sullivan (AUS) – 47.05 sec. / **200m:** Michael Phelps (USA) – 1 min. 42.96 sec.
OLYMPIC: 100m: Eamon Sullivan (AUS) – 47.05 sec. / **200m:** Michael Phelps (USA) – 1 min. 42.96 sec.

SHORT-DISTANCE FREESTYLE

The 100m and 200m races give swimmers a chance to demonstrate speed over a longer distance.

A NEW DAWN?

~n Fraser (AUS) won the Women's
)m freestyle in 1956, 1960,
 1964. She was the first swimmer
~r to win an Olympic gold in the
~e event three times in a row.

Dawn Fraser (AUS)

SPLIT-SECOND TIMING

Swimming races are timed electronically. The signal to start the race automatically starts the clock. As each swimmer touches the wall at the end of the race, a pressure pad records his or her time to within one hundredth of a second!

GET OUT OF MY WAY!

 1920, the final of the Men's 100m
~eestyle had to be swum again after
~ Australian competitor complained
~at a U.S. swimmer had impeded him.
~owever, it made no difference to the
~sult, as both races were won by Duke
~hanamoku—a member of the
~awaiian royal family.

SUPER STATS

The pool used at the Olympic Games is 160 feet (50m) long—almost double the length of two tennis courts.

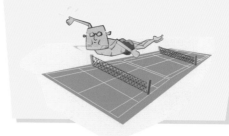

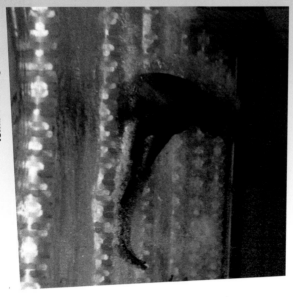

Tumble turning

MIDDLE- & LONG-DISTANCE FREESTYLE

The longest races are also freestyle events. These are the 400m, the Women's 800m, and the Men's 1,500m.

WAY TO GO

The 400m freestyle is twice as long as the longest race in any other single stroke.
The Men's 1,500m is the longest race of all, though—an incredible 30 lengths of the Olympic pool! It takes great stamina, as well as great speed.

STROKE OF LUCK

These days, all freestyle swimmers use the front crawl, but in the past, competitors have used other strokes. In 1904, Emil Rausch (GER) won the gold in the 1 mile freestyle using the

ABOUT TURN

Freestyle swimmers use a technique called the "tumble turn" to spin around at the end of each length. Just before they reach the wall of the pool, they do half a somersault. They push their heads under the water and twist their bodies around to face the other way. Then they use

Kieren Perkins (AUS

& TWO RECORDS

Kieren Perkins (AUS) set an Olympic record in the 1,500m at the 1992 Games in Barcelona. Two years later, he set a new world record in the event. Further success came in 1996, when he won another gold medal at the Games in Atlanta.

ANIMAL OLYMPIANS

When it comes to long-distance swimming, blue whales are tops. Every year, they swim up to 12,427 miles (20,000 km) — nearly twice the distance between Great Britain and Australia!

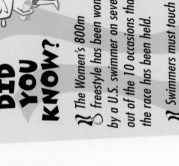

WOMEN'S RECORDS – WORLD: 400m: Federica Pellegrini (ITA) – 4 min. 01.53 sec. / 800m: Rebecca Adlington (GBR) – 8 min. 14.10 sec.
OLYMPIC: 400m: Federica Pellegrini (ITA) – 4 min. 02.19 sec. / 800m: Rebecca Adlington (GBR) – 8 min. 14.10 sec.

BREASTSTROKE

Competitors in the 100m and 200m breaststroke are always looking for loopholes in the rules that will enable them to swim faster. Now the breaststroke has more regulations than any other stroke has.

HANDY ADVICE

Breaststroke swimmers must touch the side of the pool with both hands at the end of every length. Failure to do so means instant disqualification!

SUPER STATS

The breaststroke is the slowest stroke. The fastest breaststroke champion has a top speed of just 3.73 MPH (6 km/h). You could run about three times as fast.

HEADS UP

About 30 years ago, breaststroke swimmers discovered that they could swim faster under water. So a new rule was introduced, which says that their heads must break the surface on every stroke—except at the start of the race or when turning.

MEN'S RECORDS – WORLD: **100m**: Kosuke Kitajima (JPN) – 58.91 sec. / **200m**: Kosuke Kitajima (JPN) – 2 min. 07.51 sec.
OLYMPIC: **100m**: Kosuke Kitajima (JPN) – 58.91 sec. / **200m**: Kosuke Kitajima (JPN) – 2 min. 07.64 sec.

WHAT A DIVE!

All swimming races (apart from backstroke events) start with the competitors diving off of the starting blocks and into the pool. A good racing dive is shallow and powerful. Breaststroke swimmers often dive slightly deeper than competitors in other strokes do, as they are allowed to swim their first stroke under water.

Racing dives

DID YOU KNOW?

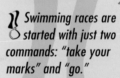

Swimming races are started with just two commands: "take your marks" and "go."

In 1936, the bronze medal in the Women's 200m breaststroke was won by Inge Sörensen (DEN). She was only 12 years old at the time!

If the Men's 100m freestyle champion had a race with the 100m breaststroke champion, he would win by more than 10 seconds!

BREAST EFFORT

In the breaststroke, the swimmer's arms and legs stay under water. Both arms move together in a circular motion, stretching out in front of the swimmer, then pushing down through the water and coming back underneath the chin. At the same time, the swimmer kicks his or her legs like a frog.

FLYING THE FLAG

Backstroke swimmers can't actually see where they are going! A row of flags is hung across the pool, 5.47 yards (five m) from each end, to warn swimmers they are getting close to the pool wall. When turning, swimmers can use any part of their bodies to touch the wall.

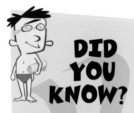

DID YOU KNOW?

An Olympic swimming lane is 8.2 feet (2.5m) wide.

The fastest swimmers go in the middle lanes; the slower ones get the outside lanes.

The floating lane dividers stop swimmers from bumping into each other and reduce the waves that are created by the swimmers.

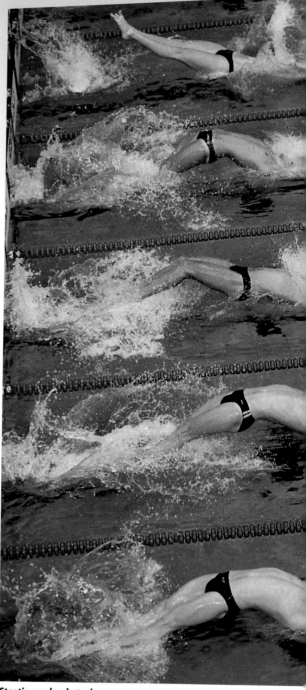

Starting a backstroke race

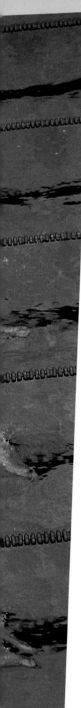

BACKSTROKE

The key to success in the 100m and 200m backstroke is to keep your body as straight as possible.

RECORD COLLECTION

Dawn Fraser isn't the only swimmer to win three Olympic golds in one event. Kristina Egerszegi (HUN) won the 200m backstroke event three times between 1988 and 1996, and holds five golds in all. At the 1992 Games in Barcelona, she also set two new Olympic records when she won both the 100m and 200m.

Kristina Egerszegi (HUN)

CRAWLING BACK

In the backstroke (or "back crawl"), swimmers must remain on their backs at all times except when turning. The leg action is the same as in the front crawl. The arms move one at a time in a circle over the swimmers' heads and through the water.

WET START

Instead of diving off of the starting blocks, backstroke swimmers hold on to a rail along the edge of the pool and lean back with their knees bent and their feet against the wall. When they hear the starting pistol, they launch themselves backwards by pushing off the wall with their feet.

ANIMAL OLYMPIANS

Sea otters often swim on their backs, too. In fact, they can even do it in their sleep!

MEN'S RECORDS - WORLD: 100m: Kirsty Coventry (ZIMBABWE) - 58.77 sec. / **200m:** Kirsty Coventry (ZIMBABWE) - 2 min. 05.24 sec.
OLYMPIC: 100m: Kirsty Coventry (ZIMBABWE) - 58.77 sec. / **200m:** Kirsty Coventry (ZIMBABWE) - 2 min. 05.24 sec.

BUTTERFLY

The butterfly is the newest Olympic stroke. The 100m event was introduced in 1956 for women and 1968 for men; the 200m was held for the first time in 1968 for women and 1956 for men.

ANIMAL OLYMPIANS

The massive manta ray is the butterfly champion at the Animal Olympics. It swims by beating its giant fins like underwater wings.

BALANCIN ACT

Swimmers need to be very strong, especially butterfly events. Howe if their muscles becom too big, they are unab to move smoothly and their swimming techni is affected.

Denis Pankratov (RUS) won the gold in both men's butterfly events at the 1996 Games.

FLOAT LIKE A BUTTERFLY

butterfly is the hardest stroke to master. Swimmers
ng both of their arms through the air, then pull them
n through the water. At the same time, they move
r legs in a "dolphin kick," keeping their feet
ether while moving them up and down.

Inge De Bruijn (NED) is the current Olympic and World champion, winning both titles at the 2004 Games. She has eight Olympic medals overall, including four golds. Here, she is pictured winning the Women's 100m butterfly at the Sydney Olympics.

DID YOU KNOW?

Although almost all butterfly swimmers use the dolphin kick, they may also use the breaststroke kick.

The 200m butterfly world record held by Mary Meagher (USA) is 21 years old—the oldest world record ever.

Kristin Otto (GDR) became the only person ever to win gold medals in three different strokes when she won the Women's 100m butterfly, backstroke, and freestyle in 1988.

VERY IMPRESSIVE

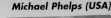

Michael Phelps (USA) has been a champion swimmer since the age of 15, when he broke the world record in the 200m butterfly. He is currently the world record holder in the 200m butterfly, the 100m and 200m freestyle relay, the 200m and 400m medley, the 200m freestyle, and the 100m medley relay. He holds the Olympic record in the 100m butterfly. Phelps has won 14 Olympic gold medals, eight of which he won in the 2008 Beijing Olympics.

DID YOU KNOW?

🏊 Tamas Darnyi (HUN) is the only person to have won both the 200m and 400m medley events at two Olympic Games.

🏊 An indoor pool was first used at the Olympics in 1948. Until then, races had been held outside.

🏊 Competitors can be disqualified if the judges think that their swim suits are too skimpy!

FOUR-STROKE POWER

The medley is a four-stroke race. Competitors must use a different stroke to swim each quarter of the race, in this order: first the butterfly, then the backstroke, then the breaststroke, and finally, the freestyle.

CHILL OUT

According to Olympic regulations, the temperature of the water in the pool should be between 77°F (25°C) and 80.6°F (27°C), which is slightly cooler than most public swimming pools.

MEN'S RECORDS – WORLD: 200m: Michael Phelps (USA) – 1 min. 54.23 sec. / **400m:** Michael Phelps (USA) – 4min. 03.84 sec.
OLYMPIC: 200m: Michael Phelps (USA) – 1 min. 54.23 sec. / **400m:** Michael Phelps (USA) – 4 min. 03.84 sec.

MEDLEY

In the 200m and 400m individual medleys, each competitor must use all four different strokes.

CLOSE ENCOUNTER

The narrowest victory in Olympic history occurred in 1972, in the final of the men's 400m medley. Gunnar Larsson (SWE) beat Tim McKee (USA) by just two thousandths of a second — a distance of 0.12 inches (three mm)!

SUPER STATS

The current Olympic records in both the men's and the women's 400m individual medleys are now more than 30 seconds faster than the winning times when the races were first held in 1964 — that's long enough to do another length!

BANNED!

elle Smith (IRL)

At the 1996 Games, Michelle Smith (IRL) won gold medals in the 200m and 400m individual relays, plus a gold in the 400m freestyle and a bronze in the 200m butterfly. However, her glory at the Olympics soon turned to disgrace when she failed a drug test and was banned from taking part in future competitions.

RELAY

Teams of four swimmers each swim a quarter of the race in the 4x100m freestyle, 4x200m freestyle, and 4x100m medley relays.

CLEAN SWEEP

Historically, the U.S.A. has dominated the relays. At the 1996 Atlanta Olympics, U.S. swimmers won every one of the six races. The Women's 4x100m freestyle team set new Olympic records in 1996 and 2000, only to be beaten by the Australian team in 2004.

1996 US women's 4 x 100m freestyle team

SUPER STATS

There have been a total of 80 relay races held at the Olympics. The USA has won 55 of them.

MEDLEY MIX

In the medley relay, each member of the team uses a different stroke. The first swimmer swims with the backstroke, the second with the breaststroke, the third with the butterfly, and the fourth swims freestyle.

MEN'S RECORDS – WORLD: 4x100m fr.: USA – 3 min. 08.24 sec. / 4x200m fr.: USA – 6 min. 58.56 sec. / 4x100m m.r.: USA – 3 min. 29.34 sec.
OLYMPIC: 4x100m fr.: USA – 3 min. 08.24 sec. / 4x200m fr.: USA – 6 min. 58.56 sec. / 4x100m m.r.: USA – 3 min. 29.34 sec.

SWIMMING APEMAN

400m freestyle relays in 1924 and 1928 were
n by the team from the USA. One of the members
hat team was Johnny Weissmuller, the greatest
mmer of his day. He won a total of five Olympic
ds, and eventually went on to become a famous
vie star — by playing Tarzan in Hollywood movies!

*Johnny Weissmuller
as Tarzan*

WAIT FOR IT!

During relay races, each swimmer must wait
for his or her teammate to touch the wall
before diving in. If a swimmer starts too
soon, the whole team is disqualified.

DID YOU KNOW?

The U.S. men's teams have won the 4x100m freestyle eight out of the ten times that it has been held.

Eleanor Holm (USA), who won the 100m backstroke in 1932, starred as Tarzan's girlfriend Jane in a film that was made in 1938.

The oldest person to win a medal in any swimming event was 46-year-old William Henry (GBR), who won a bronze in the 1906 freestyle relay.

DIVING

Diving has been part of the Olympics since 1904. At the 2000 Games, two new synchronized diving events were introduced.

TAKE FIVE

There are five basic types of dive, known as forward, backward, reverse, inward, and twist. However, there are more than 100 recognized variations. Divers try to impress the judges by performing gymnastic moves, such as somersaults and twists in mid-air.

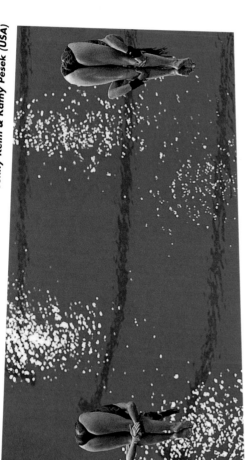

Jenny Keim & Kathy Pesek (USA)

IT'S A SYNCH!

Synchronized diving is when two divers perform together. The idea is that both divers mirror one another as closely as possible, and they are then judged as a pair. There are springboard and platform synchronized competitions.

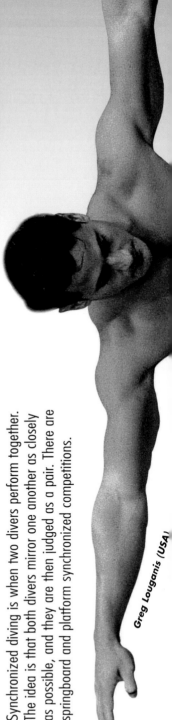

Greg Louganis (USA)

There is no such thing as a world or Olympic record for diving.

While attempting a reverse dive at the 1988 Olympics, Greg Louganis (USA) hit his head on the springboard and was badly injured. However, he refused to pull out of the competition and, with his head still in bandages, went on to win his fourth Olympic gold medal!

SPRING INTO ACTION

Olympic diving competitions include both springboard and platform events. The springboard is just 9.8 feet (three m) above the pool and is very flexible. By jumping on it, competitors can spring high into the air. You can find out about platform diving on pages 22–23.

ANIMAL OLYMPIANS

At the Animal Olympics, the sperm whale would win the diving by 1.5 miles (2.4 km). That's how deep these huge creatures can dive in search of something to eat.

This is because the scoring system has frequently changed, so events can't be compared.

DIVING
(CONTINUED)

The platform dive takes strength, courage and balance.

NEED A HAND?

Here, 1996 Olympic platform champion, Dimitri Sautin (RUS), is shown performing an armstand dive, which is only made from the platform. Competitors start by doing a handstand at the very edge of the board, then push off with their arms.

ANIMAL OLYMPIANS

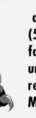

As platform divers hit the water, they are falling through the air at up to 34.2 MPH (55 km/h). When peregrine falcons dive down on their unsuspecting prey, they reach speeds of 217.5 MPH (350 km/h).

GOLDEN AGE

At the 1996 Games, then 17-year-old Mingxia Fu (CHN) was the fourth female to capture both the platform and springboard events. In 1990, she became the youngest ever world diving champion — at the age of 11! Since then, the rules have changed; now all divers in both world and Olympic competitions must be at least 14 years old.

There is no such thing as a world or Olympic record for diving.

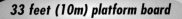

33 feet (10m) platform board

25 feet (7.5m) platform boards (not used in Olympic competitions)

16 feet (five m) platform boards (not used in Olympic competitions)

9.8 feet (three m) springboards

A jet of water causes tiny ripples on the surface of the pool underneath the diving boards. Without it, the divers would not be able to see where the water began.

JUDGE & JURY

individual diving events are judged by a panel of seven
ges. Nine judges score the synchronized dives. The
nber of points per dive is awarded as follows: first, the
ges mark each dive out of 10 for performance; then they
tiply their scores by a number according to the difficulty
he dive—the harder the dive the higher the number.

DID YOU KNOW?

Klaus Dibiasi (ITA) won the platform competition in 1968, 1972 and 1976—the only Olympic diver to have won the same event three times in a row.

The platform dive is also known as the "highboard"—for obvious reasons!

The first Olympic diving competition for women was held in 1912.

GAME ON

Each water polo match consists of four seven-minute quarters and there are two referees to ensure fair play. The pool must be 98.4 feet (30m) long, 65.6 feet (20m) wide, and at least 5.91 feet (1.8m) deep. The court is marked out with lines that are painted on the bottom of the pool.

DID YOU KNOW?

🏊 The first-ever Olympic water polo tournament was won by the Osborne Swimming Club from Manchester, representing Great Britain.

🏊 A member of the winning Hungarian team in 1932 and 1936 had only one leg.

🏊 In 1968, the team from the German Democratic Republic beat their opponents from the United Arab Emirates by 19-2: a record score!

TOUGH PLAY

To play water polo, competitors need the stamina of a long-distance swimmer, the accuracy of a quarterback, and the strength of a wrestler.

There is no such thing as a World or Olympic record for water polo.

WATER POLO

Water polo was first played at the Olympics in 1900. It was the only team sport at the early Games apart from soccer.

POLO CRAZY

Water polo is a bit like an aquatic version of soccer. Each team has seven players, and the idea is to score as many points as possible by throwing the ball into the opposition's goal. Players may only use one hand when passing or shooting, and no one except the goalkeeper is allowed to touch the bottom or sides of the pool.

Men's water polo

SUPER STATS

Hungary has won the Olympic water polo tournament more times than any other country, with eight victories to its credit. Great Britain is second with four wins, while Italy and the former Yugoslavia share third place with three wins each.

HUNGARY	ⅢⅢ I
GREAT BRITAIN	ⅢⅠ
ITALY	Ⅲ
YUGOSLAVIA	Ⅲ

COLORFUL CAPS

Players wear colored bathing caps to show which side they are on. Usually, one team wears white and the other blue. Goalkeepers usually wear red caps. The caps have ear protectors as well as chin straps to stop them from being pulled off.

This is because the objective is to win rather than to achieve as high a score as possible.

WATER POLO
(CONTINUED)

Water polo was a male-only sport at the Games until the 2000 Sydney Olympics, when women were allowed to compete for the first time.

ONES TO WATCH

Italy's women's team was the winning team in the 2004 Olympics when it beat the Greek team 10-9. The only other Olympic match for women in 2000 was also close, with the Australian team beating the USA 4-3.

SUPER STATS

Water polo players can often swim up to 3.11 miles (five km) during a match.

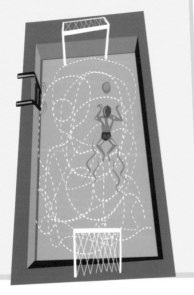

BLOCK TACTICS

When defending, players try to block the other team's shots using their arms and bodies. By kicking furiously with their legs (remember, they are not allowed to touch the bottom of the pool), they try to leap out of the water in front of the attacker just as he or she throws the ball. It takes great strength—and great timing!

GET OUT OF THE POOL

Water polo is a rough, physical sport, but players are not allowed to dunk or hold on to each other. Fouls can result in players being sent out of the pool for 45 seconds; three such offenses usually means that they stay out for the rest of the match!

FREE THROWS

As in soccer, if the ball goes out of play (in this case, if it lands outside the pool) the team that touched it last is penalized, and the other team is given a throw-in. Free throws are also awarded in the event of a foul. If a serious offense is committed by one side, its opponents are given a free shot just 13 feet (four m) away from the goal.

reen O' Toole) & Gillian len Berg (NED)

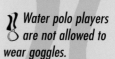

DID YOU KNOW?

Water polo players are not allowed to wear goggles.

In addition to the two referees, there are several other officials whose job it is to watch out for fouls.

Each team is allowed to make four substitutions during a match.

WATER MUSIC

Speakers in the walls of the pool enable the competitors to hear the music while they are under water. This makes it possible for swimmers to move together with split-second timing.

Synchronized duet

DID YOU KNOW?

🎵 The synchro duet was held in 1984–1992, but not at the 1996 Olympics.

🎵 In 1992, the winners of both the gold and the silver medals were twins: Karen and Sarah Josephson (USA) won the gold, and Penny and Vicky Vilagos (CAN) the silver.

🎵 Japan has won medals in the duet event in every Olympic final!

GOLD OLGA

Canada and the United States have been the traditional winners in the synchronized events. However, in the last three Olympic Games, Russia has come out on top, winning both the duet and team events. Olga Brousnikina (right), shows how it's done.

SYNCHRO DUET

Synchronized swimming (or "synchro") appeared as an exhibition event at the Olympics in 1948–1968, before becoming a full medal sport in 1984.

BEAUTY TIPS

Competitors use waterproof lipstick and make-up to help them look their best. Instead of wearing a swimming cap, some swimmers put gel in their hair. This means that their hair stays perfectly in place, even under water!

SHALL WE DANCE?

Synchro began in Canada in the 1920s and was originally called water ballet. Like ballet, it involves moving to music, but instead of dancing, competitors perform in water. Only women are allowed to compete in synchro, which makes it the only swimming discipline with no men's event.

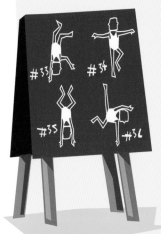

SUPER STATS

There are nearly 200 different recognized moves in synchronized swimming. So if you practiced four moves a week, it would take you almost a whole year to learn them all.

SYNCHRO TEAM

The synchro team competition was introduced at the 1996 Olympics. Each team is made up of eight swimmers.

PART ONE...

Both the duet and the team events are made up of two parts. The first is a technical routine, where competitors must perform specific moves in a certain order and within a set time.

...AND PART TWO!

The second part of the competition is a free routine without restrictions. This gives the swimmers a chance to show off their skills with as much creativity as possible.

Synchronized swimming team (N

ANIMAL OLYMPIANS

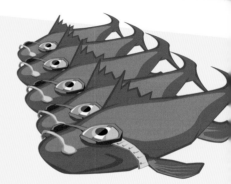

Herrings are the synchro swimming champions of the animal kingdom. They swim together in huge groups (called "schools"), sometimes comprising several million fish, with each one following almost exactly the movements of the rest.

WINNING BY A NOSE (CLIP)

nose clip is the most essential piece of equipment that synchro
immers need. It prevents water from entering their noses, helping
m hold their breath and stay submerged longer. Competitors are
o allowed to wear a swimming cap and goggles, if they wish.

Synchronized swimmer

MAKING YOUR POINT

Two panels of five judges award points for each part
of the competition. One panel scores the execution
of the moves — how well they are performed. The
other panel scores the overall performance — how
beautifully the different moves are linked together.

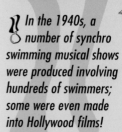

DID YOU KNOW?

In the 1940s, a number of synchro swimming musical shows were produced involving hundreds of swimmers; some were even made into Hollywood films!

Boosts, rockets, thrusts, and twirls are all names for different synchro moves.

Until 1992, there was also a solo synchro competition for individual medalists.

SILVER: SPAIN   **BRONZE:** CHINA

INDEX

COUNTRY ABBREVIATIONS

AUS – Australia
BEL – Belgium
CAN – Canada
CHN – China
DEN – Denmark
ESP – Spain
EUN – Unified team (Commonwealth of Independent States, 1992)
FIN – Finland
GBR – Great Britain
GDR – East Germany (1949-90)
GER – Germany

HUN – Hungary
IRL – Ireland
ITA – Italy
NED – Netherlands
RSA – South Africa
RUS – Russia
SWE – Sweden
USA – United States of America